THE
BALANCING
ACT

The Balancing Act

A *Counting Song*

Illustrated by
Merle Peek

CLARION BOOKS
TICKNOR & FIELDS: A HOUGHTON MIFFLIN COMPANY
New York

For the McCulloughs
David, Fran, Ben, and Katy

Clarion Books
Ticknor & Fields, a Houghton Mifflin Company
Lyrics and music of "One Little Elephant Balancing" from *Sally Go Round the Sun*
by Edith Fowke. Used by permission of the Canadian Publishers, McClelland
and Stewart Limited, Toronto, copyright © 1969.
Text and illustrations copyright © 1987 by Merle Peek.

Library of Congress Cataloging-in-Publication Data
Peek, Merle.
The balancing act.
"Lyrics and music of 'One little elephant balancing'
from Sally go round the sun [collected and edited]
by Edith Fowke"—T.p. verso.
Summary: One elephant after another strides onto
the high wire until there are ten and the wire threatens
to break.
[1. Counting.   2. Songs.   3. Elephants—Fiction]
I. One little elephant balancing.   1987.   II. Title.
PZ8.3.P2763Bal   1987   [E]   86-17547
ISBN 0-89919-458-3

Printed in Japan

DNP   10 9 8 7 6 5 4 3 2 1

1

One little elephant balancing,
Step by step on a piece of string.

He thought it was such an amusing stunt
That he called in another little elephant.

2

Two little elephants balancing,
Step by step on a piece of string.

They thought it was such an amusing stunt
That they called in another little elephant.

They thought it was such an amusing stunt
That they called in another little elephant.

4

Four little elephants balancing,
Step by step on a piece of string.

They thought it was such an amusing stunt
That they called in another little elephant.

Five little elephants balancing,
Step by step on a piece of string.

They thought it was such an amusing stunt
That they called in another little elephant.

6 Six little elephants balancing,
Step by step on a piece of string.

They thought it was such an amusing stunt
That they called in another little elephant.

7 Seven little elephants balancing,
Step by step on a piece of string.

They thought it was such an amusing stunt
That they called in another little elephant.

8

Eight little elephants balancing,
Step by step on a piece of string.

They thought it was such an amusing stunt
That they called in another little elephant.

9

Nine little elephants balancing,
Step by step on a piece of string.

ELEPHANTLAND
ARENA

TODAY
10 [COUNT THEM] 10
ELEPHANTS
BALANCING
⋆ A ⋆ C ⋆ T ⋆

They thought it was such an amusing stunt
That they called in another little elephant.

Ten little elephants balancing,
Step by step on a piece of string.

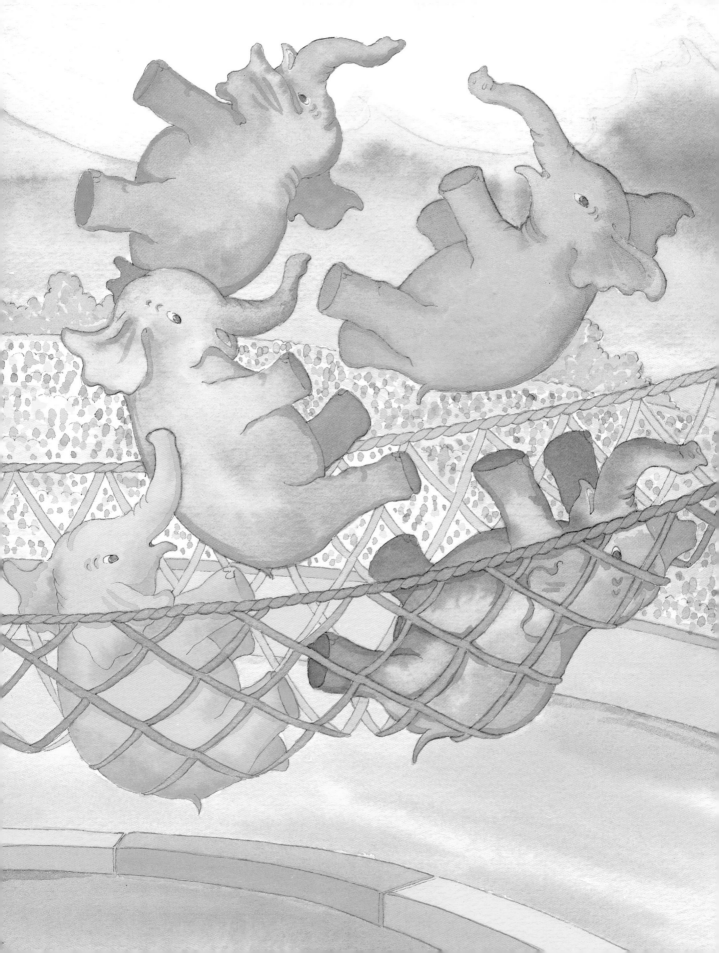

A Note from the Author

This song may also be used as a game. Make a large circle with string or chalk on the ground or floor. The size of the circle is determined by how many players there are—the more players, the bigger the circle. The players all sit outside the circle, and a leader is chosen.

While everyone sings, the leader walks on the circle. The leader holds his nose with one hand and puts his other arm through the opening made by the arm which is holding his nose. This makes an elephant trunk and will also make for very nasal singing which will be funny.

At the end of the first verse, the leader points to another "little elephant" who joins in the circle and holds on to the leader with his or her "trunk." At the end of the second verse, the second "little elephant" chooses another to join in. Each new "little elephant" holds on to the one in front with his or her "trunk," and at the end of the verse chooses the next one to join in. This continues until everyone has joined the circle; it's not necessary to stop at ten if there are more players.

When the last "little elephant" joins the circle, the string "breaks," and all the players drop to the ground. Then the last player chosen becomes the new leader, and the game begins again.

One Little Elephant Balancing

One lit-tle e-le-phant ba-lan-cing,
Step by step on a piece of string. He
thought it was such an a-mus-ing stunt That he
called in a-no-ther lit-tle e-le-phant.

Two little elephants balancing,
Step by step on a piece of string.
They thought it was such an amusing stunt
That they called in another little elephant.

Three little elephants balancing,
Step by step on a piece of string.
They thought it was such an amusing stunt
That they called in another little elephant.

Four little elephants balancing...